ADVENTURES OF Moxie Mouse

Written and Illustrated by

Dürten Kampmann

Getting as far away as possible from his current neighborhood was foremost on the mind of Moxie the mouse. The situation with Ping-Pong the cat had reached a point were he barely dared to venture out of his mousehole. Having made up his mind to move, he decided to leave with a bang.

Knowing Ping-Pong's habit of creeping along the same plank of the old dock each morning trying to catch the kingfisher, Moxie had a brilliant idea. Helped along by dry-rot and his mousy know-how, he managed to weaken the plank to the point where Ping-Pong didn't stand a chance.

Before Ping-Pong knew what hit him, he was splashing in the icy water. It was great! Moxie found that revenge was not only sweet, it was delicious. However, now that he had truly burned his bridges he had to find a new place to live. By doing some serious scouting he found a home that he thought had all the right stuff, including…

3

A standard poodle named Bella and her mistress Willapa. Willa and Bella are best buddies. Willa is the owner of a 1965 VW bug named Mabel inherited from an aunt. Mabel's long life is the result of many engine and other body-part replacements, but otherwise she hasn't changed much. Moxie built a fluffy nest under Mabel's hood and brought in a supply of birdseed he found in the garage.

One day while filling Mabel's gas tank, the attendant pointed out to Willa, "Ma'am do you know that you have a mouse living in your car?" "Yeah, a cute little guy," said the lady in the SUV next to them, looking down from her car window. That was that. Back home, Moxie was evicted. This was just as well because the same day all manner of bags and bundles were stored where his bed used to be. Apparently a trip was in the making. Moxie knew just what to do.

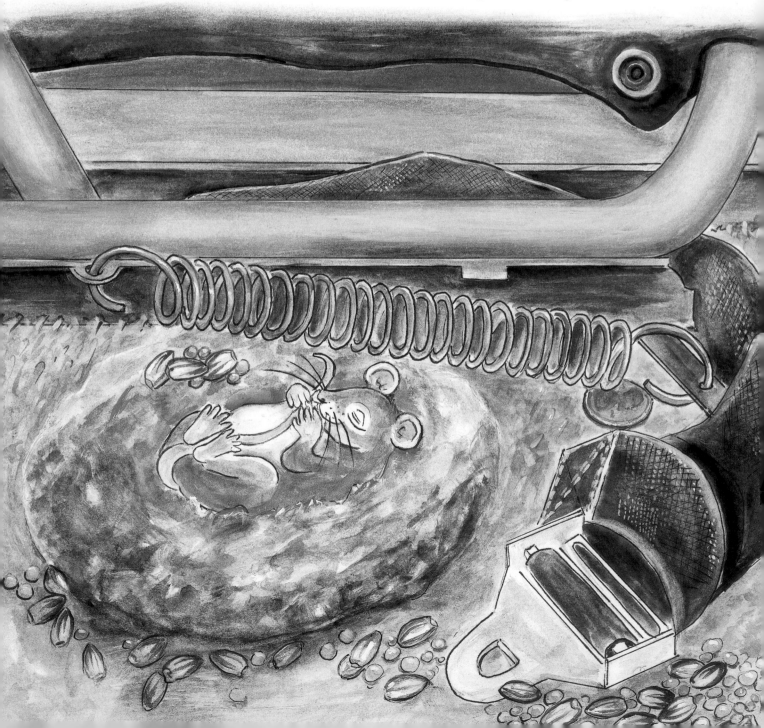

Moxie moved his stuff under the front seat, right where all the action was. He was very tidy and arranged everything just so. It was a good move. His new digs were heated and had wall-to-wall carpeting. Finally, he could relax.

The next morning Willa, Bella, and Moxie were driving down a country road to explore wherever their fancy would take them. Moxie had settled in well and was looking forward to the adventure.

They spent the night behind an old barn. The next day they found a bright yellow boat and decided to take it out on the lake. Bella thought it was more

sporting to dig for a mouse in the wild than the one right under her nose and watched from shore. Moxie who was always ready to try something new, decided to treat himself to an exiting sea trip with Willa. Anchors aweigh!

After putting the boat back where they found it, they moved on. Mabel's backseat had been removed and replaced with a foam mattress to give Bella more room to roll around. It also made a comfortable spot for Willa to take a nap.

During afternoon siesta time, Moxie worked hard to fluff up his pad with some of Mabel's insulation.

11

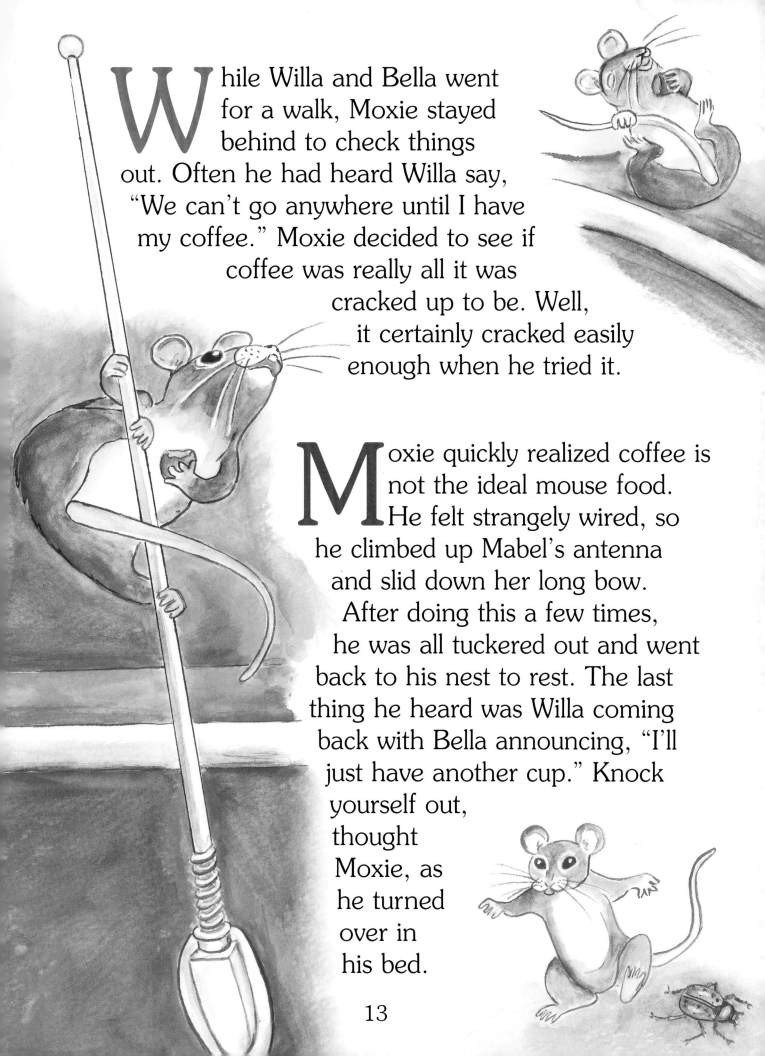

While Willa and Bella went for a walk, Moxie stayed behind to check things out. Often he had heard Willa say, "We can't go anywhere until I have my coffee." Moxie decided to see if coffee was really all it was cracked up to be. Well, it certainly cracked easily enough when he tried it.

Moxie quickly realized coffee is not the ideal mouse food. He felt strangely wired, so he climbed up Mabel's antenna and slid down her long bow. After doing this a few times, he was all tuckered out and went back to his nest to rest. The last thing he heard was Willa coming back with Bella announcing, "I'll just have another cup." Knock yourself out, thought Moxie, as he turned over in his bed.

13

M oxie was snoozing comfortably in his new and improved digs, when he was woken by loud rat-tat-tats and drumrolls. The big woodpecker on top of their car was very happy. Mabel did not quite have the beautiful tone of a metal gate, but he was hoping his message would be heard. To protect their ears from his latest tune, our gang quickly pulled up camp. Followed by the bird who felt another opus coming on.

E ver optimistic, Willa concentrated on weaving Mabel through all the potholes along the country roads. She didn't seem to notice the cougar tracks as big as dinner plates on the road, though Bella and Moxie both picked up a distinct catty odor in the air. Soon the potholes got bigger; some even had entire ecosystems of salamanders and pollywogs living in them. Still they were making good time driving through the woods when suddenly disaster struck…

Mabel's
rear
end
got stuck in the
mud when Willa tried
to turn the car around on
a logging road that seemed
to go nowhere. Excavation began
immediately. Bella went into her alert watchdog mode. Willa
jacked up the car and with the help of Bella's water dish
began filling the hole under the tire with gravel from the road.

Moxie wanted to help. His digging skills came in handy
as he rolled stones under the wheel. This is how they
built the pyramids, Moxie thought. He had a hunch
that a stuck tire wasn't their only problem.

18

Their team effort paid off. Just as night fell, Mabel was freed from the mud. Soon they found a great place to pitch camp and settled down for the night and some much deserved sleep. Finally, it can be revealed, the cougar was just as happy to see the last of them.

Morning found them on a bluff overlooking the sea. After last night's harrowing events, everyone felt relaxed, each with pleasant thoughts. Moxie could tell that Mabel was feeling like a prince this morning. As the day wore on, the ocean breeze beckoned. Since it was such a gorgeous day, they all went for a walk on the beach.

Moxie had no idea the world was so big. He remembered the small river he used to live on. This was nothing like it. The ocean stretched on forever. As each wave rolls ashore anything can happen. It may bring objects washed from boats, or the shores of distant countries. Or it might sneak up on you and make your feet wet.

24

Cars were allowed on this part of the beach. When the tide is out the sand is packed tight and firm. Willa and Bella loved the ocean. Moxie took it all in. He was in awe of a flock of stately birds, looking like poetry in motion, flying overhead. Just in case, and because he was a take-charge kind of guy, he took cover under the ramparts of an abandoned sandcastle. But all went well.

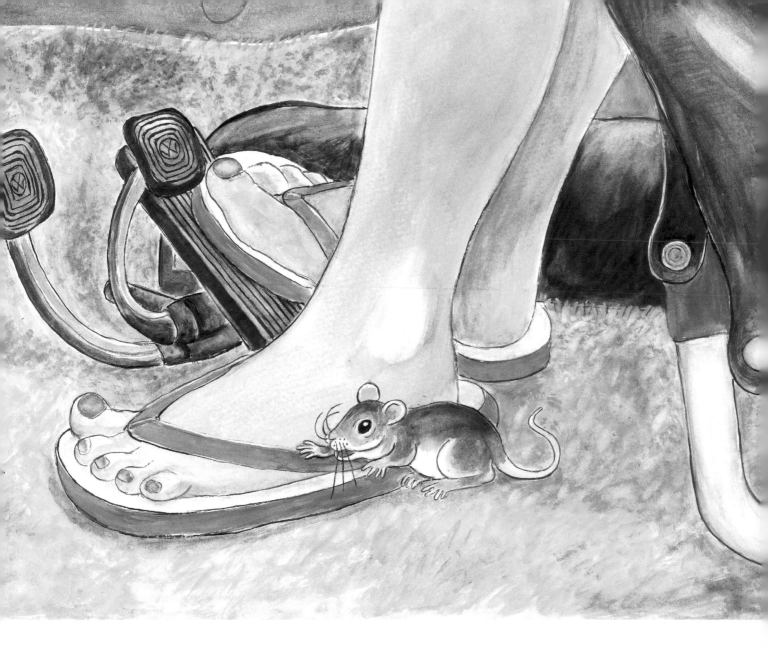

Mabel and the gang left the sea behind and headed back into the mountains. Maybe to do some fishing. Back home, Moxie had become an efficient under-the-seat driver. He could tell from the way Willa's toes curled if something exciting was afoot. He would immediately dash up onto the back of the passenger seat to look out the window. This time it was an inviting rocky pool. Willa, who could not pass a mountain stream without checking out its swimming holes, wasted no time testing this one. Bella cased out the local wildlife while Moxie admired the scenery.

Every curve in the road brought something new. Ping-Pong and his other old problems seemed far away now. Today Moxie went sightseeing up an ancient oak tree. Not for the first time he was thankful that everybody's prey of choice was salmon. Clearly fish were being caught here. Willa got one too, though not as big as the osprey's whom they first met on the lake behind the old barn. Now here she was feeding her chicks—the accomplished professional.

Willa was beginning to think of home and Bella was wondering if all her hiding places were still secure. So, to the sound of distant, peaceful splashing in the stream they turned the car around. Moxie, riding shotgun on the backrest, leaned into the curves. Somehow he knew they were heading back to the barn.

Finally they were back home, the best place of all. Looking forward to their next adventure!